Darby Down Under

Written by
Barbara Massey
and
Sylvia DeLoach

Illustrations by
Amy Giles Robinson

New Hope® Publishers
Birmingham, Alabama

New Hope® Publishers
P.O. Box 12065
Birmingham, AL 35202-2065
www.newhopepubl.com

Library of Congress Cataloging-in-Publication Data

Massey, Barbara.
  Darby down under / by Barbara Massey and Sylvia DeLoach.
    p. cm. -- (A child like me)
Summary: While in Australia with her grandparents to see the Olympic
games, twelve-year-old Darby visits the Great Barrier Reef, sees koalas
in a zoo, and meets some famous athletes.
  ISBN 1-56309-766-4
  [1. Grandparents--Fiction.
   2. Olympics--Fiction.
   3. Australia--Fiction.]
I. DeLoach, Sylvia. II. Title.
  PZ7.M4237 Dar 1999   [Fic]--dc21   99-050762

Cover design and illustrations by Amy Giles Robinson

ISBN: 1-56309-766-4
N007107 • 0599 • 3M1

Br—ring! Br—ring! sounded Darby's alarm clock. *No! It can't be 5:30 A.M. already,* thought Darby groggily, as she rolled out of bed.

Yes it is, she thought again, as she heard Grandmom moving around the kitchen.

Darby pulled on her warm-up suit, laced her shoes, and grabbed her gym bag.

"Morning," she said, as she went into the kitchen and saw her grandparents already enjoying a cup of coffee.

"How's our favorite gymnast?" asked Grandpop, with a smile curling his lips.

"Ready for my workout," replied Darby, as she reached for the glass of orange juice Grandmom had poured.

"Remember, Darby," reminded Grandmom. "Today's Wednesday and that's the day we always call your mom and dad to let them know how you're doing."

"That's right, Grandmom," answered Darby. "I'm glad they finally agreed to let me live with you and Grandpop this year while I train with Coach Sanders.

He is a great gymnastics coach. I really, really want to try for the next Summer Olympics. You know I'll be 13 then."

"Come on, Darby, I'll drop you off at the gym," said Grandpop.

"And, Darby, don't forget to remind Coach Sanders that we will be in Australia next week," said Grandmom.

"Oh, I won't forget, Grandmom," replied Darby. "I still can't believe I'm getting to go see the real Olympic Games," she added, as she picked up her gym bag and headed for the car. "This will be a dream come true!"

Northern Territory

Western Australia

Queensland

South Australia

New South Wales

•Sydney

Victoria

Tasmania

"Almost perfect," said Coach Sanders, as Darby completed her routine on the balance beam. "We'll work some more on this when you get back from Down Under. That's what Australia is called, you know."

Tossing Darby a towel, Coach Sanders added, "There's one place I'd like you to check out while you are in Sydney. It's the Australian Institute of Sports."

"I can *guess* what that might be," answered Darby. "But what exactly is it?"

Coach Sanders explained. "Several years ago the Australian government decided it wanted its athletes to do well in international sports competition. They began the Institute to train coaches. In fact, I know a coach at the Institute in Sydney. His name is Coach Loft. And listen to this, Darby, he trains gymnasts."

"Oh, I have to go there," said Darby. "And I want to meet Coach Loft. But how can that happen?"

"No problem, Darby. I've already thought about that. I'll email him today and tell him to expect you and your grandparents," said Coach Sanders.

"Thanks, Coach," said Darby. "See you when I get back! Down Under, here I come!"

Darby's eyes opened wide as she gazed out the airplane's window. "We're here, Grandmom," she said, hardly able to contain her excitement. "I thought this day would never come!" Darby's eyes darted over the city of Sydney and as the plane prepared to land she cried, "There's the Sydney Opera House, Grandpop! Look!"

"Darby, it looks just like it did on our computer when we took the virtual tour," responded Grandpop. "I can almost hear that harpsichord concert. Wonder who's appearing there now?"

Darby and her grandparents began their first full day in Sydney by making a stop at the Australian Institute of Sports. "I'm so glad we came early so we can get a taste of Australia before the Olympics begin," said Darby. "And I'm glad Coach Sanders told us about this place," she added as they walked up to the Institute. "I hope Coach Loft has a minute to see us."

"You must be Darby Day from the United States," said a friendly-looking man who approached Darby and her grandparents as they entered the Institute.

Darby's face broke into a huge smile as she shook hands with Coach Loft. "Coach Loft, these are my grandparents who made this trip possible for me."

As Coach Loft greeted Grandmom and Grandpop, he said, "I'm glad to meet you. I understand Darby is living with you so she can train in the sport she loves.

I want to thank you, because it takes a whole family to make an athlete. Let me take the three of you on a tour of our Institute. And I also want to introduce you to someone special who is here today."

"Conner!" called Coach Loft. "Come meet some friends from the US."

"Conner, meet Mr. and Mrs. Day and their granddaughter, Darby," continued Coach Loft. "Darby is a gymnast, too."

"*G'day, Mates!*" responded Conner in his friendly Australian way.

"I thought you'd enjoy meeting someone who is really competing in the Olympics," said Coach Loft.

Darby's eyes were fixed on Conner and her mouth was wide open. When she was finally able to speak, she said, "Really? You are really an Olympic gymnast?"

"I am," answered Conner. "And this is my first year to compete. I'm an official member of the Australian Olympic Team—the Stars of the Southern Cross!"

"What does that name mean?" questioned Darby.

"Well, have you seen the Australian flag?" asked Conner. "The stars on the flag represent the constellation of the Southern Cross. Wait a minute, I'll show you." He reached in his back pocket and took out a small Australian flag. "Here," he said, handing it to Darby and smiling. "You'll need this while you are here. Welcome to Australia!"

Before leaving the Institute, Darby and her grandparents agreed to meet Conner and Coach Loft for a trip the next day to the Great Barrier Reef. Darby had studied the reef in school and could hardly wait to go.

"I've never been on a glass-bottomed boat before,"
Darby said, as she boarded the boat and began their day's
adventure at the Great Barrier Reef.

"Wait until you see all the exotic fish," said Conner,
"like the Moorish Idol, the Butterfly Fish, and my
personal favorite, the orange Clownfish. They find
protection in the reef among the rocks
and plant-like animals called *anemones*."

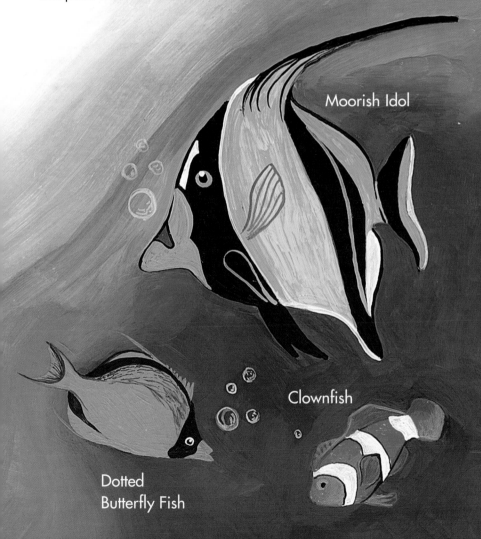

Moorish Idol

Clownfish

Dotted
Butterfly Fish

"Look at all the beautiful colors," observed Grandmom. The coral was in vivid shades of purple, pink, yellow, and red. "These formations look like a huge bed of flowers."

"Exactly!" replied Coach Loft. "That's why the Great Barrier Reef is sometimes called the Underwater Garden."

"How did all this happen?" wondered Darby aloud.

"Oh, I know the short answer to that," said Conner with a grin. "Because the water is always warm, tiny marine animals called polyps grow and produce coral. Basically what happens is these polyps secrete a form of calcium which hardens into limestone.

This is what the coral reef is made of. More than 300 kinds of polyps grow and they come in many different colors."

"Good job, Conner," said Coach Loft. "A scientist might explain this with more detail, but that description was pretty good for an athlete."

"I learned a lot today," said Darby as they returned to Sydney.

"We all did," added Grandmom.
"What an unusual day!"

"One more Australian treat before we part for the day," said Coach Loft. "Conner and I want you to experience the favorite national dessert in Australia."

"We'll all have *pavlova*," Conner said to the waiter in the restaurant. "You will really like this," he said to his new friends.

"What is *pavlova*?" asked Darby.

"It's a fruit-topped cream filling in a meringue shell. And it's good!" answered Conner. "I even know why we call it *pavlova*. It was named after the world famous Russian ballerina Anna Pavlova to honor her on her first visit to Australia."

"Yum! This is good! I can see why this is everybody's favorite," said Darby, as she took her first bite.

The next day as Darby, Grandmom, and Grandpop took the ferry to the Taronga Zoo, Darby had one thing in mind. "I can't wait to see a real koala," she said excitedly.

"I hope we can see lots of new things," replied Grandpop.

"Well, as Conner would say, we'll take a *Captain Cook* at everything!" answered Darby. "That means 'take a look' in Aussie talk."

"Let's read this sign before we go in," suggested Grandpop, as they arrived at the zoo.

Grandpop began to read: "Welcome to the Taronga Zoo, world's best international zoo. Home to more than 3,000 animals from all around the world."

"Oh, look, Grandmom and Grandpop," said Darby. " Read this sign. I can have my photo taken with koalas while we are here. For free! I can't wait to show that to my friends back home!"

The day at the Taronga Zoo had been quite an adventure for Darby, Grandmom, and Grandpop. On the ferry back to Sydney, Darby pulled out a small tablet on which she had written the names of the animals she had seen. "Let's talk about what we liked best at the zoo. Grandpop, you go first," she said.

"Well, I'll say Serpentia, the reptile and amphibian exhibit. I'll never forget seeing the frill-necked lizard. What a funny-looking creature when he puffs out his neck like a pleated fan! I feel like I've seen a 'real Australian' since this lizard is found only in Australia," said Grandpop.

"We saw
another 'real
Australian' in my
favorite part of the zoo,"
added Grandmom. "The duck-billed
platypus. It reminded me of the platypus
we saw at the Great Barrier Reef. Now, Darby,
it's your turn."

"No question about this," began Darby. "I have two things. I'll
never forget seeing the koalas eating their favorite food, euca-
lyptus leaves. And it was so much fun to go through the kanga-
roo, wallaby, and emu area."

As Darby put the tablet in her backpack, her fingers brushed against the surprises she had bought at the zoo for her friends back home. "I think Kristen will love this boomerang," said Darby. "Don't you think it's interesting, Grandpop, that the boomerang used to be a weapon. And now it's a toy?"

"You're right," replied Grandpop. "Early Australians used the boomerang for hunting."

"I like the boomerang better as a toy," added Darby.

"This is the best trip of my life, and today's the best day of the trip," said Darby as she awoke early on the day of the opening ceremonies for the Olympic Games.

"Remember, Grandmom and Grandpop, this is red, white, and blue day," she added as she bounded out of bed.

"In all of our red, white, and blue we will look like the US flag," said Grandpop.

"No one will have to guess who we are cheering for," laughed Grandmom. "And I'm glad we each have our own little American flag to wave when our team enters the arena," she added. "I get goosebumps just thinking about it."

"That reminds me," said Darby, "Conner gave me a little Australian flag. It looks like I'll have two teams to cheer for today."

"I've never seen this many people before," Darby said wide-eyed, as they took their seats for the opening ceremonies.

"I've always enjoyed watching the Olympics on television," said Grandpop. "But there is no way to catch the excitement like being here."

"Seeing all the different people from all different cultures makes it seem like the whole world is here," added Grandmom.

"They're starting," whispered Darby, as she watched groups of athletes waving their countries' flags and beginning their march around the stadium.

"Watch closely, Darby," said Grandpop with a twinkle in his eye. "You may have to do that one day."

"We will definitely be in the stands watching," added Grandmom. "And you don't have to wonder what colors we will be wearing that day!"

"Look," exclaimed Darby, "there's the Australian flag with the Southern Cross constellation! It's time to wave my flag for Australia's team, the Stars of the Southern Cross. Grandpop, may I borrow your binoculars? I want to find Conner."

Darby scanned the group of athletes. "There he is, wearing the green and gold!" Darby said excitedly. "Conner told me all Australian children dream about being chosen to wear Australia's green and gold, the national colors, in international competition. And he's getting to wear them!"

"As the Aussies would say, 'Carn, Conner!' Do you know what that means, Grandmom?" asked Darby. "It's the Aussie way of saying, 'Come on, Conner!'"

At the end of the day, Darby could not believe all she had seen. Her mind filled with thoughts of becoming an Olympic gymnast. She pictured herself on the balance beam, poised before the crowd. *I can do it!* she thought.

"I'm going to practice harder than ever," she told Grandmom and Grandpop. "Conner gave me some great tips. I can't wait to tell Coach Sanders."

"Well, you'll get to do that this week, Darby," said Grandmom. "Vacation is over. You'll soon be back in your familiar routine—up at the crack of dawn and off to the gym you'll go!"

"I'm not going to mind a bit," Darby said smiling. "Olympics, here I come!"

The Sydney airport buzzed with excitement as Darby, Grandmom, and Grandpop went through customs. What a trip this had been—koalas, kangaroos, and best of all, the Olympics. Darby hugged her stuffed koala as she walked with Grandmom and Grandpop through the airport, tired but very happy.

"Look at the television cameras," said Darby. "Why are they here? Let's find out."

"What's going on here?" Grandpop asked someone in the crowd.

"Oh, we are seeing our Australian Olympic team off," replied the friendly man. "We are so proud of our athletes."

"There's Conner!" said Darby, waving her Australian flag and hoping he would see her.

"Darby," called Conner, as he noticed his new friend in the crowd. "Come over here and join us!" Darby could not believe her eyes and ears.

She made her way through the crowd and when she reached Conner's side, he said to his team members, "Give a listen, mates. This is my new chum, Darby. She came to the Sydney Olympics as a spectator, but I think we will be competing against her in the next Olympics in Athens."

"*Carn*, Darby!" the Australian Olympic team cheered. "See you in Athens!"